MISSION 49

BY: SIYANA KEDIR

MILTON & HUGO L.L.C.
4407 Park Ave., Suite 5
Union City, NJ 07087, USA

Website: *www. miltonandhugo.com*
Hotline: *1- 888-778-0033*
Email: *info@miltonandhugo.com*

Ordering Information:
Quantity sales. Special discounts are available on quantity purchases by corporations, associations, and others. For details, contact the publisher at the address above.

Library of Congress Control Number:	2024923492	
ISBN-13:	979-8-89285-290-6	[Paperback Edition]
	979-8-89285-289-0	[Digital Edition]

Rev. date: 11/11/2024

To my mom and dad
for always being there for me.

☆ AUDIO TEXT MESSAGE ☆

Kronos
Wednesday, April 25, 2:30pm

Good afternoon Mr. Ways, I have assigned you a new mission. Mission 48. I need you to retrieve something valuable for me. It is a silver necklace with a green pendant. It once belonged to me. But now, it's in the hands of Juniper Tree. If you do not retrieve the pendant within twenty minutes, the bombs surrounding Ms. Trees' house will go off. Come back in one piece.

Kronos, head of SCSS, "I have eyes everywhere."

☆ Attacked by Deer's ☆

Okay, so being attacked by deer's isn't the best start for a mission. Especially if it's from the boss himself.

Suddenly, I came to a dead end. "Shoot." I murmured underneath my breath.

They cornered me.

"Look, I don't want any problems! Just let me go and I'll be on my merry way." I tried to confront the deer's but they just sneered.

"We hate when humans walk on our territory." The deer on the right side said.

Oh, did I forget to mention that these deer's can talk? Yeah, so apparently a while ago some scientists did an experiment on the deer's and now they can talk.

Not like they used their mouths to say anything good anyways.

A bigger deer with large antlers made its way through. It was as if all the deer's scattered aside to let it through.

Its beady eyes watched every move I made and examined me. At last, it finally stated, "I see you are part of the SCSS."

My hand rose up to touch the arm tag that boldly printed out SCSS. I stood up straight. "Yes. I do."

The deer turned around and said something in *Deerish* to the rest of the deer's. I couldn't understand what they were since I didn't have my Polyglot reader on me but I picked something up.

We can't afford another loss.

What did the head of the deer's mean by that?

The same stubborn deer that had spoken to me earlier still had a tinge of annoyance in his voice as he answered, "the boss said to let you go."

I waited for the deer's to move before I could run away. But one caught me in the ribs with its antlers.

Although it jabbed my ribs, it hadn't hurt but instead grazed my hand and in seconds, blood gushed out of the wound.

I wasn't prepared to have gotten hurt so I hadn't had a First Aid kit equipped.

I quickly tore a leaf from a tree and used it as a temporary gauze for the bleeding.

It hadn't hurt but the blood said otherwise.

The "boss" deer had still been lingering behind.

He stood still for a moment then uttered, "child, be careful of Kronos." He cautioned.

Before I could reply, he had run off to catch up with the pack.

Thoughts bubbled up but before I could overthink about what he said, my virtual assistant, Bitzy buzzed.

She was on my watch, my phone and all my gear. It sounds pretty neat until she blabbers about stupid things.

"T-minus ten minutes until bombs go off, Miles. Be prepared." She buzzed. Her voice had a hint of femininity but it was mostly robotic.

The bleeding had gone down a bit but it would still leave my hand with a long thin scar.

I tugged my sleeve down to hide the scar. If dirt or too much air got on it, it would get infected.

According to Bitzy's GPS, I would only have to walk a few more minutes until I pulled up to Juniper's house.

It was funny because she lived on the edge of the woods.

It became harder and harder to navigate through the trees but I finally came to a clearing where a house made of bricks was standing.

I carefully stepped up. This wasn't a raid. Simply a trade. 10k for the necklace. I rang the doorbell.

It took a few seconds but a woman with dark hair, pale skin, green eyes opened the door.

She narrowed her eyes. "Can I help you?"

"Are you Miss Juniper Tree?"

She nodded, still looking suspicious.

"I work for a government agency called SCSS and–"

As soon as she heard the name, she almost shut the door in my face. I quickly held the door open. "Please talk to me, Miss Tree."

"Please leave. Now." She said, still trying to close the door. I held it with a firm grip.

"I'm here to make you a trade. Ten thousand dollars in exchange for that." I nodded over to the silver pendant around her neck.

"No… you're not getting your hands on this." With a last shove, she slammed the door closed. Even with my fast instincts, I wouldn't have been able to catch it.

"Miss Tree, please, let's talk. Ten thousand is a lot of money. Could get you out of this dump."

"My house isn't a dump, thank you very much." She hissed from behind the door.

I tried to reason with her for the next five minutes until Bitzy gave me the final minute warning I began re-thinking this mission.

To make sure I was safe.

I sighed. "What about 100k? Please think about that." I was willing to negotiate but 100k was a lot of money. Money that she could buy a whole new necklace with. A *better* necklace with.

The door was still shut but I knew she was behind the door.

I glanced between my watch and the door. Was Kronos really going to harm someone because of a necklace, no matter its significance?

"Bitzy, turn off the bomb."

She answered almost immediately. "Turning off bombs."

I trudged away, I had saved her life but did that mean sacrificing mine?

It was just a stupid pendant, with all the money Kronos had, he could buy a better one.

The walk back was worse than the walk to. The sky was dark and it seemed like it could rain any minute. Thankfully, my suit had a heater and was water-proof and could easily protect me from nature's harm.

The rain started pouring down and I broke down in a run, passing by the deer's and into my car.

I slammed the door closed and got in. I sucked in a breath. I had to prepare myself from Kronos' wrath.

I quickly drove back but the weather got worse and worse. By the time I reached the headquarters it was almost completely dark and thunder boomed somewhere in the distance.

I parked the car in the garage and rushed into headquarters. The first level was just the reception room because after all the outside world thought we were a tech company.

In reality though, SCSS was a government agency that did little...missions for the government.

 Little missions that the public didn't know about.

I leaned down so that our AI advisor, Aimee, could scan my eye. "Welcome, Miles Ways."

The door automatically opened and I entered the elevator. "Level three please." I commanded.

There were no buttons inside the elevator and it was completely controlled by my voice. The elevator dinged and shot up to the third level.

The layout of the headquarters was simple. First floor, reception, where normal people would come in and get their devices fixed by our "tech" company.

Second floor was the "tech" company's workspace, where we had our younger spies, who weren't quite old enough for missions, fix the devices. Of course, no normal person was allowed on any floor other than the first. Kronos made sure of that.

Third floor, which had security measures inside and outside of the elevator, was the glass reception room for spies. Where they'd report after their missions to catalog their items and add notes to CloudNotes which would be stored in the cloud where Kronos would look if he had any questions about the mission we went on.

Fourth floor was the biggest floor, the spies dorms. There were sixty spies ranging from seven years old to nineteen years old. The fourth level had everything you needed. There was even a private pool, balconies in each room, and vending machines in every hall. Four spies would all share a big dorm which was the size of a small one-story house.

Fifth floor was Kronos' and Natalie's office. Kronos, the head of SCSS was often in his massive glass office with his treasured assistant's office right next to his. Everything on the fifth floor was glass and also rare for you to go up there.

Sixth floor was a more classified floor which only certain spies could go in - thankfully, I was one of them but most spies never needed to go up there unless something was wrong.

The seventh floor is still a mystery for me. I knew it existed but that was it. I had tried to pry information out of Aimee but for a robot, she was pretty smart. I even offered her a new upgrade but she refused.

Aimee had a nasty attitude these days so even the short elevator rides with her ticked me off. More than Bitzy.

Aimee had rambled about something about how I hadn't respected her by taking off my shoes whenever I came into "her" elevator.

Although Aimee was AI, she felt *very* real. Finally, I reached the third floor and stepped out.

Our virtual assistant, Jules, who ran the third floor greeted me. "Good afternoon, Miles. What can I do for you?" Jules was a newer AI so her voice had feminine sound. Kronos had even managed to hook her up with emotions, where she could distinguish what other people were feeling.

"I'd like to turn my gadget in and put some notes on CloudNotes, please." I said, taking out my gadget, the invisibility cloak, which I hadn't used because Juniper hadn't even let me talk.

Jules took the cloak and it quickly disappeared into the Gadget Portal. I pulled out my phone and opened CloudNotes. A hologram appeared in front of me. I started typing on the holographic keyboard noting that Juniper had been stubborn and unwilling to negotiate. Of course, I didn't put that I hadn't retrieved the necklace.

I closed out CloudNotes and the hologram disappeared. As I turned to leave, Jules stopped me.

"Miles." She paused, a slight electric sound coming from her. "Where is the necklace?"

I froze. I had been hoping she didn't notice. She often glitched but today she was fine. "I gave it to Natalie." I lied.

"That is incorrect." Bitzy buzzed from my watch.

Oh no, she didn't. Bitzy was *so* getting shut down after this. "Yes, I did. Bitzy is glitching."

Jules paused again. "Liar." She said, finally. "The necklace is not in the system. This is now a failed mission. Exporting to Kronos…"

"W-wait!" I tried to stop her but a ding interrupted me. She had already sent it to Kronos.

"Could I do anything else for you, Miles?" Jules asked, innocently.

"No, you've done enough." I trudged over to the elevator and hit level four.

"Have a good rest of your day, Miles." Jules chirped and she whirled back to silent-mode.

As the elevator opened, I ran a hand through my hair.

I was *so* cooked.

☆ Discussions ☆

I headed to the infirmary first, to get my wound bandaged up properly.

The bleeding had stopped not too long ago but blood still covered the scar. Thankfully, there were no AI robots in the infirmary and instead it was one of the spies that were there.

Today it was a spy I hadn't really known well but we got along and she bandaged my hand up and I headed to my dorm.

My roommates Taj, Mae and Tala were playing Uno on the floor. I had just come in when Taj had screamed Uno.

"Miles, my boy…guess who won Uno?" He said, running up to me and slinging an arm around my shoulders.

I shrugged off his arm. "Not now, Taj." I slumped over to my bed and hit my pillow, face-first.

"What happened now?" Mae asked, rolling her eyes. She had been pissed off because she had bet Tay that she would win Uno.

I told them what had happened with Juniper and how Jules had marked it as a failed mission.

Tala, who had stayed quiet, fiddled with her ring. "You do know that Kronos had told you that if you failed one more mission…"

"Yeah, I know." *There would be a consequence.*

Almost on cue, Bitzy buzzed back to life. "Miles, Kronos needs you to report to his office immediately."

We all shared a knowing look and I got up with a huff. "See you guys later."

When I entered the elevator, I really wasn't in the mood to deal with Aimee. Although I technically wasn't supposed to do that, I shut her down. Temporarily of course. The next spy could always turn her back on.

Not that the only thing she did was be a resident chatterbox. The elevator still operated perfectly fine without her.

To my surprise, after I shut her down, she whirled back to life. "Now, that wasn't very nice of you, Miles." Her fem-robotic voice chirped. "Must be hard failing a mission."

I rolled my eyes. "Bitzy, is it possible for me to kill an AI?" I asked my watch.

"No. That is impossible because an AI is not a real person therefore—" Bitzy started.

"Bitzy, power down."

"Powering down…" My watch went dark.

Ugh. Living in a world like 2060 wasn't as amazing as everyone thought it would be.

The elevator dinged to the fifth floor, Kronos' and Natalie's office.

The entire floor was made of glass and I hated coming up there. The walls were glass, the desks were made out of glass…it made me sick to my stomach.

Natalie looked up from her desk, positioned in front of the elevator. "Good afternoon, Miles. Kronos will be with you shortly." She gave me a tight smile. "Till then, please feel free to sit and read a magazine."

I nodded and quickly sat down on the leather couches. Of course, next to it was a glass table piled up with magazines, word crosses and tablets.

I picked up a magazine and started reading. I came across a page about the deer's I had met earlier and how more and more poor animals are getting tested on.

I remembered what the Alpha deer had said to me earlier. "Natalie, do the experimented deer's have something to do with Kronos?"

She glances over at me. "No, why?"

9

I shrug. "Just asking."

Natalie pauses before going back to her computer.

She had been a bit suspicious but I stayed quiet. The deer had said be careful of Kronos, not Natalie after all.

Shortly after, a kid named Bently Yalmat stumbled out of Kronos' office.

He looked pretty shaken and I didn't ask why.

Natalie cocked her head towards the Kronos' door. "Go in, he doesn't bite."

Ha. I doubt that. Still, I gave her a small smile before knocking and entering his office.

Kronos' was sitting at his big glass desk with a computer and papers on top. He looked up and his piercing blue eyes made eye contact with mine.

Kronos had jet black hair, icy cold blue eyes and pale skin. His cheekbones were prominent and high and he had a tall, built figure.

Without saying anything, he gestured to the white and silver chairs in front of his desk.

I slipped into the one closest to the door. In case, I had to, y'know...dash.

Kronos' eyes fell on me and his eyes quickly scanned me. Kronos had the ability to do that. Where he could see my emotions, my body temperature, heart-beat and those sorts of things. "Are you nervous?" He asks, finally.

His voice is deep and velvety and it quietly echoes in the large glass room.

"Yes, sir." I couldn't lie even if I wanted to.

He nods. "The necklace is reported missing. Jules scanned it as a failed mission. Has she been glitching?"

I swallowed. Hard. "No, sir."

He raised an eyebrow. "So where is the necklace?"

I chuckled nervously. "Well, you see, sir...Juniper wasn't willing to negotiate. No matter the amount of money I offered her."

He cocked his head to the side and narrowed his eyes. "And?"

"She wouldn't let me in and I couldn't use my invisibility cloak because she would have gotten suspicious." I took a breath. "I didn't retrieve the necklace, sir."

Kronos didn't say anything for a bit. "Mr. Miles, do you remember the conversation we had not too long ago?"

Of course. I wanted to say. It was exactly two years, fifteen days and seven hours ago. "Yes, sir."

"And you do realize that we have consequences for failed missions?"

"Of course, sir. And I promise it'll never happen again!" I pleaded.

His eyes locked with mine for a second and I felt a chill down my spine. He looked away a moment later and he pulled something out of his desk drawer. It was a pocket-knife.

I froze.

His eyes almost looked amused at my fear but that wasn't possible. Kronos doesn't show emotion. He *couldn't* show emotion.

"If you remember, Miles, we have a three strike chart. Your first strike was three years, ten days and twenty three hours ago when you failed Mission 25. Do you remember?"

"Yes, sir." Although for a regular person it would be hard for someone to remember the precise day, hour and minute that something happened, but everybody at SCSS, including me, somehow had photographic memory.

"Second strike was two years, five days and three hours ago. When you refused to go on a mission due to cold weather."

I looked down. "Yes, sir." I had been thirteen at the time and I hadn't quite understood how important the "strikes" were.

He starts tracing lines on his hand with the knife. "This was your last strike."

"I promise, sir, it will never happen again."

Kronos paused and he reached over. I almost flinched. But if there was anything I learned at SCSS was to never show fear.

Never let the enemy know he affected you in some sort of way.

Kronos' hand brushed my cheek and he looked at me with something I could only describe as....affection. "Miles, did you know you were one of the very few spies that almost always complete their missions without a fuss?"

I nod. It wasn't always like that, but I switched up. For the better.

He moved away. "That's why I'm giving you one last chance." He paused before slicing the pocket knife against the palm of his hand. "Next time, you'll receive more than a warning."

I freeze in horror, as his thick red blood trickles down and splattered onto my jeans.

He throws the pocket knife back on his desk and sits down. "Well, enjoy the rest of your day, Miles."

I nod my head quickly. "You too, sir."

"Oh and Miles?" He says before I slip out of his office.

"Yes, sir?" I hesitantly turned back around, hoping that he hadn't changed his mind about letting me off with a warning.

"Don't be so nervous next time." His eyes once again seemed like they danced with amusement before he turned back down to his computer.

I sucked in a shaky breath and left.

Natalie looked up. "How'd it go?"

I tried to laugh the nerves away. "All good...heh."

She nodded. "That's good. Well, enjoy the rest of your day, Miles."

"You too." I headed back into the elevator and went one floor down to the dorms.

Taj, Mae and Tala were still there, Taj and Mae in another game with Uno and Tala typing away on her computer.

I walked over and sat on the floor next to Taj. "You guys start a new round yet?"

Taj clapped my back. "That's the Miles I know!" He put down a red five, "nah, we still have a few cards left."

I nodded and watched them play.

"I assume Kronos *didn't* say he was gonna kill you in your sleep?" Mae asked, putting down a red reverse card, then putting a red six.

"Ha, no. I was sweating bricks and he could tell." I tried to rub off the red blood off my jeans even though I knew it wouldn't come off.

Before either Mae or Taj could say anything, Bitzy went off and blurted, "Miles, please report to the fifth floor to receive information on your next mission."

The air turns cold. New mission?

"Bitzy must be glitching, Tal, can you fix her up?" I asked, taking off my watch and handing it to Tala.

"Yeah…" She takes my watch and starts tinkering with it but a few seconds later she stops. "Miles, Bitzy is working perfectly."

"But how? I can't have a new mission after I just flunked Mission 48!" I said, running a hand through my hair.

"Maybe it's important." Tala mumbled, handing my watch back.

"Or maybe Kronos changed his mind about killing you in your sleep." Taj elbowed me.

"Not funny." I grumbled, getting up.

I knew Taj was just kidding but a sinking feeling in my stomach felt that whatever reason I was called up for, it wasn't good.

☆ Luke Vladamiser ☆

I headed up to the fifth floor for the second time today.

Thankfully, Aimee stayed quiet throughout the four second ride.

I headed into the changing rooms to change into my suit that kept me at perfect temperatures, knew my health status and checked the weather.

I hurried over to Kronos' office, nodded over to Natalie.

To my surprise, instead of being greeted by Kronos, I went face to face with a tuft of blonde hair.

Ugh. I couldn't suppress an eyeroll. I was hoping I hadn't had to talk about him. Luke Vladamiser.

Most people in these types of stories have mortal enemies, I wasn't like that up until a few years ago when Luke joined SCSS.

Luke was evil, conniving, fake and twisted. I hated him.

Luke flashed me a fake smile. "Miles! Pleasure to see you."

"Same to you, Luke." He shook my hand, squeezing a bit tighter than necessary.

I took my hand back quickly. Knowing Luke, he'd be on his best behavior in front of Kronos.

Luke didn't look like much more than an average boy with fair skin, dirty blonde hair and icy blue eyes. We were about the same height although Luke would like to argue otherwise.

Luke had come to SCSS not too long ago and only had his break-through three months ago when he had brought Aimee. I couldn't even believe he was assigned such an important mission although he was a newbie.

Still, I congratulated him which he had brushed off and called me jealous. Ever since then, we had been on bad terms. I never knew why he hated me and I never asked. As long as he didn't interfere with my life, I didn't care what he was doing.

Kronos nodded. "Great, you're here, Miles. I'd like to introduce you to Mission 49," he looked over at me and then to Luke, "and mission 26–for you, Luke."

We nodded. I suppose we were going on a mission together. Out of the sixty spies in SCSS, why Luke? I tried to hide my annoyance and focused on Kronos.

"You will be sent to the time 2065, five years from now at an archaeological site where they're holding *the* key."

My eyebrows raised. *The* key? They key to the ancient land that they called…America?

America was the land people lived in until 2030 when the government could no longer withstand, so many had scattered into Europe which still stands to this day.

Kronos nodded. "Yes, this is a very crucial mission. You must go undetected and be *very* careful. You two are my most experienced spies - even at your age – so every minute, every second you stay there, counts."

Me and Luke nodded hard. The pressure was *on*. "Yes, sir."

Kronos nodded back. "We have your suits that keep you warm, cold, temperate and always keeps you safe and of course, your gadgets." He tapped the air and to a normal person, he would have looked crazy, flinging his arms everywhere but we *weren't* normal, although we couldn't see exactly what Kronos was doing, we knew he was opening up the void and soon, he pulled two gadgets out of thin air.

To my surprise, he handed me a rope. I took it blankly. The rope was just a normal rope. "Sir, what could I possibly do with a rope?"

"Simple but useful." He noted and handed the memory eraser to Luke.

Luke gave me a smug look as he placed the eraser into his pocket.

I looked away. I knew Kronos could sense the tension but if I had to look at Luke's smug face one more time…

"This will be a very easy mission, sir." Luke remarked, gloatingly.

I shook my head in annoyance. "You need to take this seriously, Luke, what if we fall into the wrong time period without a time belt?"

Kronos nodded, grabbing the time belts from the void. "Wise words, Mr. Miles. Anything could happen in the time chasm, that's why we need to be careful as we go in and out."

He handed us our time belts which were a translucent blue color with a clock in the middle. We strapped it onto our waist and it vibrated.

"Stay together, don't move in the chasm, stay hidden and most importantly come back with the key." His eyes wandered our faces but stayed on mine for longer, noting what had happened earlier.

"Yes, sir." Luke and I replied, almost immediately.

Kronos nodded. "Come back in one piece." His eyes did that thing where they seemed to dance in amusement one last time before we spun the clock on the belt five times.

Soon, the world turned blurry and then dark.

When we opened our eyes, we were in the time chasm. To an ordinary person, it would have looked scary. It was dimly lit and everything was a cobalt blue, in front of it was a time loop that labeled on-top of it 2030.

"Ah, it must have sent us to the wrong period, we have to find 2065…" I murmured, starting to walk around the chasm, trying to find 2065.

Luke lingered behind me for a second then began following me.

He stopped when he reached 2055.

I rolled my eyes and walked back over. "The least you can do is at least follow me and not stand there, uselessly."

Luke chuckled. "I'm the one that's useless but you just failed a mission?"

My eyebrows raised in surprise. "How do you know about that?" I asked, defensively.

He shrugs. "Little ol' me doesn't know anything, I suppose." He crosses his hands on top of his chest.

I rolled my eyes for the hundredth time that day. "Okay, whatever, can we please just find 2065 so we can finish this mission?" *Being around you makes me sick*, I wanted to add.

Luke stayed put. "You know, I wonder what would happen if somebody fell into the wrong time period with no belt. That would be *devastating*."

I nodded, impatiently. "Luke, I don't know what your deal is but you better hurry up."

"Right, of course. Well, see ya." He said, stepping closer to me.

"What?" Before I could process what was happening, I felt him give me a big push and I stumbled into the time portal.

I clenched my fists in anger. Although I couldn't see anything, as it was pitch black inside the time portal, I felt air whisking past me and it felt like a never ending drop.

I felt around my waist but I couldn't feel my time belt.

My anger only grew when I realized it wasn't there. I cursed under my breath as I closed my eyes and I soon landed and felt my feet touch solid ground.

I opened my eyes, wincing from the brightness. I was in front of headquarters and I sighed with relief.

I tugged the door open but it wouldn't budge. I looked down at my watch and saw it was 8am and SCSS didn't open until an hour later for the public.

I leaned down for Aimee to scan my eye until I realized Aimee hadn't existed yet.

I huffed and typed in the passcode on the right side of the door. It slid open.

I practically sprinted to the elevator and pressed level four. The elevator made a satisfying ding before shooting up to the four floors. I knew I should have told Kronos first but I didn't want to freak him out.

I ran over to my dorm and burst in.

Taj was playing a video game, Mae was writing and Tala was tinkering with some sort of device.

Mae looked up and cocked her head sideways. "Miles, aren't you supposed to be on a mission?"

Tala swiveled around in her chair and her eyes widened. "Woah, where'd you get that high tech suit from?"

Taj, like usual, kept his eyes glued on his phone, occasionally groaning from a loss.

I chuckled nervously. "So, don't freak out but…"

"You're leaving SCSS and never coming back so they gave you a high tech suit to make you feel better and now you're here to pack your things and go?" Tala rambled.

I shook my head, more confused than upset. "No…" I paused to try to gather my words together. "Hypothetically, what if I told you I'm *not* Miles?"

They completely ignored the hypothetical part and rolled their eyes. "You are Miles! You look like him and sound like him!" Mae replied.

"Or, he could have an evil twin named Kilometer. Get it? Because his name is Miles and the opposite of miles is–" Taj chimed in but I interrupted.

"No, Taj, I don't have an evil twin and kilometers are not the opposite of miles…" I pressed, sounding a bit annoyed.

"So…what is it?" Tala asked, finally.

"I am Miles…just from the future." I answered, knowing it sounded hard to believe.

They all paused for a second and even Taj's game music glitched for a second before going back to its cartoony *do-do-do* sound.

Mae sucked her teeth. "Woah, I didn't think Kronos' actually did it…" She whispered it so low, I could barely hear.

I looked over, confused, but I didn't say anything, instead I looked over at Tala to see her reaction.

"It's possible." She nodded. "What time period?"

"2060…" I explained the story to them and they listened, thankfully, without interrupting. "…So, I just rushed over here to see if you guys could help me."

"Why didn't you go to Kronos? He might have an untested time belt for you to get back to 2060…" Tala grabbed her tablet and started typing, "of course, it'll be dangerous but it could be your only way back home."

"Guys, can we talk about the bigger problem?" Taj asked, pausing his game and turning to face us. "The guy - whatever his name is - who pushed you into the time chasm definitely wants you gone."

We all nodded in unison. "It was Luke." I noted.

Mae laughed. She paused. "That blonde newbie caused you a lot of trouble." She added, seriously.

I shrug looking down. "It is what it is, our only option now is to find a way for me to get out."

"But what will you do if past Miles comes back?" Mae asked.

"I'll just hide. I mean, I've got, what, twenty minutes till he comes back." I look down at my watch.

"It won't be good if you stay long." Taj shakes his head. "Things will get complicated. We can barely manage one Miles, two Miles is a different story." He says, trying to make a joke.

I barely offer him a smile but he was right. I needed to get back to my time period. Surely, they'll know I'll be missing, interrogate Luke and bring me back. No biggie. This could be a little vacation. A home away from home.

"What makes Luke so *highly* in 2055 anyways? Where he has the nerve to do the thing he did?" Mae asked.

I rolled my eyes, that was the worst part. Luke was always congratulated and applauded for bringing Aimee - which was fine, of course - until he just used it as an excuse to not go on missions and rub it in my face. "He brought this high-tech AI named AI89 that basically does everything for you. She's also set up in elevators, lobbies and dorms. She's fine or whatever."

They nod. "I mean, that's pretty cool."

I frown at them, basically saying they should be on my side. With a huff I add, "She can also access all the files, update CloudNotes, have awfully boring conversations with poor spies in the elevator, basically harassing them into taking off their shoes in "her" elevator."

At that point even Taj looked impressed. But could I blame them? They've never heard of any technology like that in 2055.

"Back to the time belts," Tala added urgently, "how are you going to get back home? Wait a year until Kronos makes time belts and gives them to us?"

"Well, first off, he didn't hand the time belts off like candy, it wasn't safe–" I started.

"Yeah, yeah, but what's gonna happen to you if you stay too long? I mean, you don't belong here."

"Kronos might have an untested, dangerous version of the time belt, I have to use it to get out of here." I murmured.

"You have to try, at least…because if we don't get Miles out of here soon… there will be no Miles. Past or future." Tala spoke, finally.

We all gaped at Tala and I felt the air in the room evaporate.

"So you're saying I'm going to go...poof?"

"More like being wiped out from the face of earth." Tala mumbled, turning back to her tablet, typing away furiously.

"How much time do I have left?" I asked, my throat as dry as sandpaper.

Tala didn't answer, turning her back towards us and towards her computer.

"Tala."

"It's not important. I'll tell you when you have 10 minutes left." Tala uttered harshly.

"Tala, tell me now. I want to know." I pressed, going over to her.

She looked at me, worry etched on her face. "You have twenty four hours left."

☆ The Countdown Begins ☆

I blew a shaky breath. "One day, huh?"

Taj and Mae's eyes glanced between me and Tala. "It's okay! Twenty hours is plenty of time." Mae insisted.

"There's nothing we can do," Tala muttered, hopelessly, "the longer he stays, he'll fade away and not only him but our memories of him...with him."

Even Taj looked pale.

Mae looked at all three of us before a determined look flashed across her face. "Okay, then, we'll make the most of it."

We all nodded in agreement.

Taj cleared his throat, "why don't we check Kronos's office first?"

"That's a good idea." Mae chimed in. "If there's any time belt here, it ought to be in his office."

Mae glanced at us once more to make sure we agreed with this pity of a plan.

I was going to *die*.

Ha, being pushed into a time chasm and slowly fading away from existence was one of the worst ways to go.

My watch started beeping as if I was getting a call, startling me out of my pity party.

I groaned and tried to put it on silent mode but the watch continued to beep, louder and louder.

"What's wrong with it?" Tala asked.

"I'm not sure. Maybe it's the time affecting it." Still, I pressed the side button, accepting the call.

That was when Mae's face popped onto the tiny screen. "Miles? Why do you look so pale?"

Everyone glanced at each other, dead silent.

It wasn't until Mae called my name again I finally spoke up, "no...no reason, what's up?"

She rolled her eyes, "quit fooling around. Did Kronos actually do something to you? Like I know you were pretty upset with yourself for not getting the necklace but snap out of it."

I glanced over at past Mae. I was talking to present...or I guess future Mae right now.

"Mae, I want you to listen closely and listen carefully..." I spoke slowly, "I'm stuck in 2055 and I can't get out."

Mae's eyebrows rose. "What?"

I huffed a sigh. "Luke pushed me in 2055 without a time belt and I can't get out and if I don't soon, I'll *literally* disappear."

Tala took a moment to process what I said. "Luke was smart. He knew 2055 didn't have time belts and he pushed you in there..."

I look down, defeated. Guess I was going to die.

"But." She added. "I have an idea. Risky idea. But it's something."

Taj and past Mae scooted closer to hear.

"I was sneaking around Kronos' office a while back and I found a secret passageway. I don't know where it goes or what's in it but if there's a time belt, it's probably there."

An ounce of hope ignited in my chest. "But how do you know that it's actually a passageway?"

Mae sighed, "I told you, I was passing by–sneaking, if you'd like–and I saw Kronos' typing in the air and the wall just…slid open and he entered! It closed almost immediately."

Past Mae giggled. "Aw man, I did it! I found one of Kronos' secrets. Good job future me."

I ignored her. "Do you really think that's my ticket out?"

Future Mae shrugs. "It's the only thing we've got."

I nodded. I think we all silently agreed we needed to do this. So, I asked Mae exactly what she saw.

We all creeped out of the dorm room, thankfully, not a spy in sight.

Tala whispered, "Kronos is at a big business meeting out of town so he'll be out for at least an hour…"

I swallowed hard. At least *something* was going right today.

We scurried to the elevators and I pressed level five. The relief I felt when I realized Aimee wasn't there was like a breath of fresh air. She would have dominated us with questions like why weren't we in our dorms or why we were creeping around. Or both.

The door to the elevator slid open and we were greeted by Natalie's suspicious face.

Natalie leaned closer from her desk. "Miles? Come out…" Then she quickly added, "all of you come out."

We stepped out from the elevator and Taj began running towards Natalie, carrying a taser. "KNOCK HER OUT!"

Mae tripped him, making him fall flat on his face. "I'm okay!" He announced a second later.

Natalie's eyebrow arched. "Can I help you all?"

"I left my phone in his office earlier and I came to get it."

"Earlier? You haven't been up here in a while, Miles…" Natalie's eyes narrowed.

"I was, when you were downstairs helping a customer." I remembered this day, as I was leaving to go on a mission, I saw Natalie go down to the first floor so it wasn't a complete lie.

She paused. "Alright, I'll get it for you." She began to turn around but I stopped her.

"No, it's okay. You won't find it. It's hidden. In a nook." Before she could say anything else, I scrambled to go into his office and surprisingly she didn't follow me.

In the distance I heard Mae and Taj bombard her with silly facts and questions.

I tapped my watch and future Mae's face popped back on the screen. "Now what?"

She squinted into the screen. "Well, I saw him type something that looked like his birthday and run into a wall…"

Run into a wall?

I sighed and headed to the wall she was looking at and tried September 16 1990 and I took a deep breath, backed up and ran towards the wall.

As expected, I felt an excruciating pain in my head and nose.

"Oh, Miles, wait, sorry, I meant the wall on the left…"

"You could have told me that earlier." I rubbed my nose which hurt like crazy but I walked over to the wall on the left.

I typed in his birthdate once more, backed up and braced for a horrible impact but it never came.

In unison, future Mae and I gasped in awe.

The room was a dimly lit blue color and the walls were a creamy white. There was nothing in the room other than thousands of nooks, cabinets and hiding places.

"This is so sick." Future Mae exclaimed.

I wish I could have matched her enthusiasm. "Let's just find the time belt so we can get out of here."

"That's if it exists."

The words hung in the air, practically suffocating me. I quickly took a breath of air, trying to push away the negative thoughts.

I stepped forward carefully, checking for trap doors. You could never be too cautious with Kronos.

"Check the cabinets, try the biggest ones first." Future Mae instructed.

I nodded and began searching each cabinet, starting with the big ones like Mae said.

Nothing.

Nothing.

Nothing.

Seconds flew by and all the big cabinets on the left side were barricaded open and there was nothing in any of them.

I searched the other side, hopefully.

Nothing.

"Mae, there's nothing, let's just go back…" I mumbled, helplessly.

She gritted her teeth, determined. "Keep searching."

With a sigh, I searched the smaller cabinets.

Empty.

Empty.

Empty.

I clenched my jaw and looked on the other side.

Empty.

Empty.

Empty.

There was one last cabinet on the top and I had to stretch and get on my tippy toes to reach.

Hope sparked in my chest when I felt something in the cabinet. I quickly slid it down and grabbed it.

"Mae...I think I found it." I murmured, almost in disbelief.

It looked *much* different from the time belts now but it was a belt. And it was my ticket out of here.

I flipped it around to see paper stuck onto it.

Caution, dangerous gadget, untested and is fatal.

"Mae, do you see this?" I ask, showing her the paper.

"Miles, you don't have much of a choice. Plus, didn't you see what happens when you're in someplace you're not supposed to be?"

I looked at her, confused.

"Natalie's desk. They had renovated the fifth floor and moved her desk to the elevator. Miles, this wasn't supposed to happen until *months* later."

Take the risk with the time belt or risk more things changing?

"We don't have much time before Natalie comes in looking for you." Mae urged.

"Mae, you realize that if this doesn't work I could die, right?" I insisted.

28

"Well, either way, you have a chance of dying."

She was right, of course but I just...I didn't like this idea. We still had twenty four hours, what was the rush?

Before anything else could be said or exchanged, the wall shifted open once more and Natalie with past Mae, Taj and Tala behind her.

"DROP THE GADGET!"

☆ **We're Dead Meat** ☆

23:40:15

I froze in place.

Natalie had a shocked, pale look on her face. "I know something was off! You were supposed to be on a mission right now!"

I tried to come up with an explanation for why I was here. "It's not what it looks like, Natalie! Please let me explain!"

When she stepped closer, my hands reached for the taser on my belt. "B-back away…" I muttered although I knew I would never use it on her.

Tala's eyes widened and she shook her head vigorously.

My hands shook. I wouldn't.

I *couldn't.*

If I did, Kronos wouldn't let me see another day on earth, hurting his precious Natalie.

Natalie was his longest assistant and he had often grown fond of her and for me, one of his many henchmen, to even go *near* her with a weapon was a death wish.

Natalie put her hands up. "Look, Miles, I don't want to hurt you so I'll strike you a deal, you leave here without any complaints, I'll forget everything that happened."

The deal was *so* tempting.

That was, if my life wasn't on the line.

"I can't."

Natalie's eyebrows furrowed. "What do you mean you can't? Miles, you realize I could tell Kronos and you'd face extreme consequences? Not only for trespassing but failing another mission?"

My eyebrows raised in a surprised arc, if I failed another mission, I would get my last strike, making time move faster.

Bitzy beeped loudly, "low battery please charge. If not, please hang up the call with [Mae]."

Natalie only stared at me with more confusion. "How can you be calling Mae when Mae is right behind me?"

I chuckled nervously. "Not this Mae, another Mae…"

She ignored what I said, "how did you know this place existed?"

"I…uh…" Usually, lying was almost like a 6th sense for me but for some reason, panic was so deep in me I couldn't think of a single lie.

She stepped closer, no longer afraid of the taser, "and these clothes… they're too futuristic!" She takes my arm, feeling the leathery fabric. "Who *are* you?"

I started to blabber when past Tala stepped forward, "he's from–"

"I'm Miles' twin, Kilometer!" I blurted out.

Even Taj's jaw dropped.

I made a mental reminder to beat myself up good for that later. Kilometer? Evil twin?

Natalie's chuckle was a mix of disbelief and You're-Definitely-Lying. "Miles, just tell me the truth."

At that second, my watch buzzed. "Incoming call from [Mae.]" Bitzy announced.

"Bitzy go into sleep mode." I mumbled. My watch battery was at 5%.

"Going into sleep mode…good night Miles."

The watch turned off and as it did, a new person stepped through the wall.

It was Kronos.

Everybody held their breath, waiting for his reaction.

Kronos silently surveyed the room, his eyes a deep icy blue.

Me, backed up against the cabinets with the time belt.

Natalie just a few feet away.

Tala, Mae and Taj behind her.

All of us in a room we weren't supposed to be in.

"We're dead meat."

I wasn't sure who said it.

Taj? Mae?

I couldn't tell my heart was beating a hundred miles per second. If will has it, I wouldn't wake up to see tomorrow morning based on Kronos' narrowed eyes and tight lips.

"Natalie, *what* is going on here?" He asked, his voice sharp and emotionless.

Natalie looked down. "I'm not sure what's happening, sir." She squeezed her tablet close to her chest. "They somehow found their way in here."

"Did you let them in, Natalie?"

She paused. "Yes, yes, I did sir."

I suddenly had the urge to protect Natalie. "I…It was my fault!" I blurted.

Kronos spinned around to look at me. "You're supposed to be on a mission." He massaged his temples. "I was gone for a few hours and havoc raged across my building?"

I raised my eyes in surprise. Kronos didn't show emotion often and was usually stone-faced. "I…I got back early?"

"Miles, Natalie in my office." He locked eyes with me for a second before looking over at Taj, Tala and Mae. "I'll see you three later."

That obviously had meant *scram*! And scram they did.

As the three of them scrambled out of the secret room me and Natalie looked down at the floor like it had the secrets of the universe.

Kronos walked through the portal-wall and we followed closely behind.

I glanced over at Natalie. Her face was still and emotionless but I felt her nervousness fill the air.

"Natalie, I'd like to speak to you first. Miles, wait outside please." Kronos spoke calmly compared to earlier.

"Yes sir." I scrambled out and into the fifth floor waiting room.

I sank onto the couch and my phone buzzed inside my pocket.

My heart fluttered. It wasn't dead! Maybe I could text someone to come get me out of here before it was too late.

Just 4 Spies
Taj • Tala • Mae • Miles

I texted the future group chat.

Mae

Miles, are you alright? You're not answering my calls.

Miles

As fine as I can be with a death clock on my head I guess.

Tala

Mae filled us in and we need to do something about this. Luke just got back from the mission.

Taj

Yeah and you're gonna wanna come back, he's been so cocky it's disgusting.

Miles

Real talk, I don't know how I'm going to get out of this.

For a second there was no reply. Because no amount of sugar coating would hide the raw truth.

Just then, Natalie stepped out. She kept her eyes on the floor and avoided eye contact.

What had happened?

"Miles, come in." Kronos called.

I rushed inside and per usual Kronos was sitting at his desk. "Sit." He gestured to the chairs.

I sat down, trying to calm my heartbeat. *Kronos can sense emotions, calm down heart!*

"How'd you find it?"

I was about to play the innocent game and say, "find what, sir?" but I knew Kronos could sense lies faster than you can blink. So I told a lie that wasn't a full lie. "I was looking for my phone I had dropped earlier and bumped against the wall. Then I saw half my shoulder disappeared and I just–"

"That's not possible. The room has facial recognition and your face is not one of them." He looks at me and I can tell he's scanning my emotions. "I'll ask you again, how did you find it - and answer honestly, Miles."

I stuck my ground. "I dropped my phone in your office and accidentally bumped against the wall and I saw it was a portal to a different room."

He nods. "Alright then, let's check the footage, shall we?"

I nod. If I wasn't in deep trouble now, then I can only imagine how I'd be when he sees the footage.

Kronos types into his computer for a second before moving the computer so I could see the footage.

There I was, at first, running into the wrong wall…then the other wall and then disappearing.

I was not looking for my phone and I had definitely not "accidently" ran into the wall.

I looked at Kronos' face - his eyes - which to my surprise, did that thing that looked like he was slightly amused.

"How did you bypass face recognition?" He asks simply.

I decided to tell him the truth. Maybe he would help me. "I saw you enter your birthdate in the code and I ran into the wall and I just appeared there."

His eyebrows furrowed. "Birthdate? The password is not my birthdate."

Now it was my turn to furrow my eyebrows. "Then…how did I get in?"

Kronos looked at me as if he was studying me, trying to figure out if I was truly telling him the truth. My heart had steadied and my palms were no longer sweating. "That's the question I'd like the answer to as well."

I said nothing. How did I manage to get in? Was the facial recognition broken?

"I suppose it's broken. Otherwise there is no way you'd be able to go in." Kronos mused quietly.

I nodded. So, other than the fact I still had a chance of being murdered in my sleep, this conversation was going particularly well.

"Miles, I do not know your motives or why you wanted that gadget but I trust that you were not going to use it. So, I'll let you go." He glanced at his watch. "I have business to attend so I will see you later."

"Yes, of course, sir. Thank you." I stood up and walked out, my insides churning with a mix of joy and relief and surprise.

I quickly walked to the bathroom, trying to clear my mind when my phone pinged with a text.

240-578-998 (Maybe: Mae Mae)

Miles, are you okay?

I quickly typed back "yes" and soon enough a reply came back.

240-578-998 (Maybe: Mae Mae)

It's future Mae.

My eyebrows furrowed. Why was it an unknown number? Before I could think about it more, she sent another text.

240-4578-998 (Maybe: Mae Mae)

Luke is back from his mission. He's in Kronos' office right now probably feeding him lies about what happened.

Miles (you)

Are they sending people to get me?

She started typing then stopped.

A minute passed.

And another.

Then another.

Five minutes later, a reply came in. "No."

My heart sank. I had texted Mae over ten times and there was no response.

What had she meant by no? Why weren't they coming for me?

For a few seconds I stared at the messages in disbelief until I figured out what I had to do.

I quickly texted the present group chat.

Just 4 Spies
Taj • Tala • Mae • Miles

Miles

You guys, I'm going to need a favor. Distract Kronos and Natalie.

Taj

On it.

Mae

Don't do anything stupid, okay?

I almost chuckled. Only stupidity could get me out of this mess. I turned off my phone and waited for the building to go into chaos.

And like promised, a screech ringed from the fourth floor.

I heard Natalie's heels clicking, running to Kronos' office and they soon came out of the office and headed to the elevator.

As soon as the elevator door closed, I headed into Kronos' office. I quickly disconnected the camera, stared straight ahead into the wall and like earlier, I opened my eyes to see I was back in the blue room.

I looked back at Mae and I's texts, and she still hadn't replied.

I found the time belt once more and studied it.

It looked *so* much different from the one we had in the present. It definitely didn't look safe to use. Was I really willing to use this ticket to death?

Are they sending people to get me?

No.

It echoed around my head for a while.

And as much as I didn't want to admit it, it scared me. What kind of lies had Luke pulled?

I was going to be stuck here until I fade away.

Forever.

My hands tightly clutched the time belt.

Let's not be impulsive, I told myself. Someone had to get me eventually, right? I mean…I was worth *something*, right?

But I didn't have eventually. It was now or never. For all I know, Tala's death clock was wrong and I'd fade away from existence any second now.

I couldn't help but argue with myself. If I didn't use the time belt now, Kronos would come back inside, now I'm in the secret room and god knows what happens after that. Or, I could use the time belt and it could actually work and I'd be back home and I'd forget about everything–

I almost laughed at my delusional thinking. Even if I did make it home, I could never forget this.

My phone beeped.

"Five percent remaining. Please charge." Bitzy buzzed.

Yes, she was also on my phone. She was like…the more futuristic, more talkative version of "Siri" which they had back in the days. Instead of smart-mouthing her I smiled. "Thank you Bitzy."

"Your welcome, Miles. Would you like me to go into battery saving mode?"

"No, thank you, Bitzy. Can you call Mae Mae?"

"Calling 'Mae Mae'…" The soft sound of ringing filled the room. On the last ring, I ordered Bitzy to hang up.

I stared at the time belt. Now or never. I tied it across my waist and pressed the button. A white light blinded me and then the world turned dark.

☆ That's Not A Lot Of Time Left ☆

I opened my eyes to find myself in a completely white room.

I was on a bed and the distant sound of beeping filled the room. The bright lights hurt my eyes and I forced my eyes shut.

When I reopened my eyes, I saw Natalie's clouded gray eyes hovering over me. She sighed when she realized I was awake.

I tried to get up but pain exploded in my head. "What happened?"

"Oh, just the fact that you were in the secret room that you weren't supposed to be in and used the secret gadget that you weren't supposed to know about and passed out for 19 hours." She spoke calmly as she poured me a glass of water.

My eyebrows flew up in surprise. "19 hours?!" I felt around my wrist for my watch but it was empty.

"I took off your watch. It was malfunctioning. It had some countdown til a day?"

"I...I need it back." I mumbled, sitting up, ignoring the pain.

Natalie gently pushed me back down. "It's right here, relax." She handed me my watch from the table beside the bed I was laying on.

The countdown had 30 minutes left.

I massaged my temples. The time belt hadn't worked. But...at least I hadn't died.

"What happens when the countdown ends?" Natalie asked after a moment.

I didn't reply to that question. "Where are we?"

39

"That's not important. Are you alright?"

"I'm fine." I mumbled. I looked around. The white room was empty other than the bed and the small table next to it. Was this the seventh floor?

As if Natalie read my thoughts, she stood up from the chair she was sitting on and walked over to the door. "Stay here. I hope you can at least listen to some instructions."

I couldn't contain the annoyance in my voice. "But I have questions and I know you have answers."

Natalie paused for a second before sighing and coming over. She walked over to the bed and reached under it. A second later, she pulled a small black chip. "It's recording right now." She quietly says.

My heart dropped. Were these tiny microchips everywhere? Listening into each and every conversation?

She drops the microchip to the floor and steps on it. Hard. It shatters into pieces and she collects the small shards. "You got two minutes."

"What is this room?"

She sighs. "It's a lab. We test things here."

Like making more deer's talk. Like making poor people and animals suffer.

"Why didn't the time belt work?"

She pauses. "Time belt?"

"Yeah. Time belt."

Natalie looked over at me with an odd expression on her face. "Miles, that gadget was not a time belt."

My eyebrows furrowed. "What was it then?" If that wasn't a time belt, then my only way out of here was doomed.

She shook her head. "Miles, that was an early development of a gadget to make you invisible. It clearly was dangerous, I don't know why you would use it."

Invisible? "Then...then..." Before I could get the words out, I heard from Natalie's earpiece Kronos' voice.

"Natalie, Luke Vladamiser just came back from his mission. It seems he had brought a futuristic AI called AI89, Aimee, he calls it. I need you over here."

My jaw dropped.

Luke wasn't supposed to bring Aimee until *months* later!

What was going on?

Natalie sighed. "Well, your two minutes are up. I'll get going. Stay here and stay *put*."

I nodded although I knew I wasn't going to just *stay* here and wait for the thirty minutes to go up and I'd fade away forever and ever and—

Natalie stood up and abruptly asked, "Miles, would you like to leave SCSS?"

I paused, surprised by the sudden question. "No, not really...why?"

Natalie shook her head. "SCSS is an undercover company. The government doesn't even know half of what happens here."

"But...you're a government agency?"

Natalie chuckles. "That's what we tell spies. Everything seems so simple, you come here at a young age and leave when you turn eighteen. Kronos has no need for you after eighteen."

I stare at her in shock. "Why are you telling me this?"

"I figured you'll need it." She shrugs and reaches for the door handle. "Stay put."

41

I nod and she opens the door and walks out, closing the door behind her.

Just as she leaves, I spring up. I had twenty seven minutes left. I had to do something. Be useful. If I was going to die in twenty seven minutes then might as well die with a purpose.

I needed to find the secrets of SCSS. I knew I wouldn't be here for long but I didn't realize in only three years he'd abandon me. There were rumors about him erasing spies' memories to keep the true identity of SCSS safe but I never believed it up until now. Natalie's unexpected question, the odd room…

I clenched my fists. Kronos thinks he was some sort of all mighty savior that saved us from the streets. And he did save us. And I'm grateful to him for my life.

I didn't like talking about it too much but…most kids that worked at SCSS were either orphans or found on the streets. I was one of the fortunate people. I had been put into child care services and ran away. I ran into Kronos and after that he took me in.

I remember a few years ago, a former spy who had just turned eighteen told me something. *You're not here because Kronos' wants to help you but to help himself. Remember that Miles.*

I was too young to understand what he meant by that. Now, he is gone.

Now that I think about it, he had told me important things. His name was Luca. He had been six years older than me with blonde hair, creamy hazel eyes, and tan skin. Sort of like an older brother that looked nothing like me.

Luca was Kronos' star spy, he always went on missions and completed them no matter the task. Although Kronos says he has no favorites, his eyes always twinkled when he saw Luca. That was until Luca had turned eighteen.

The last thing he had said to me was…

Ugh. My head hurt again.

I checked my watch, and I had twenty-three minutes and ten seconds left. All this thinking wouldn't get me anywhere.

I got off the bed shakily and walked over to the door. I opened it to be greeted by a gust of wind, yet I was still inside the building.

It was freezing outside…or…inside, I guess.

I quickly adjusted my suit so that it could keep me warm.

I quietly shut the door behind me. This was definitely the seventh floor. I'd never seen this place before, but I knew I was still at SCSS.

The room I was in was the last one in the dark hallway.

I started walking, my footsteps echoing on the glass floor. The hallway was full of closed doors that seemed locked with metal chains. *What* was this floor?

I eyed a security camera on the right side of me, a faint red dot fading in and out. I couldn't turn it off, it was too high up but what I could do…

I raced towards a room labeled "maintenance" so that way I could shut off the internet so it could no longer record me.

The room was dimly lit and I felt around the wall for a light-switch. When I finally found it, I audibly gasped.

This wasn't the maintenance room…

There were cots lining the room, with little children sleeping on the cots.

The sight of them terrified me. I stepped closer, just to make sure they were breathing.

Although it was small breaths, they were breathing. Were they new recruits? But…

My head started hurting as I tried to think about when I first came to SCSS. The pain was almost unbearable, I was knocked off my feet and I stumbled into a cot, moving it.

The kid on the cot jolted awake. It was a young boy, maybe five or six years old, jet-black hair and piercing blue eyes. I stepped back.

He looked around for a moment then his eyes landed on me. "Miles Ways, fifteen years old, likes; blue, dogs, and pizza. Dislikes; pickles, Luke Vladamiser, and stinky people."

I stared at him in shock. How did he know about me when he just set eyes on me a second ago? "Um, yeah, that's me."

"Why are you sneaking around? If Kronos finds out, he'll be very upset." The child blinked slowly, his eyes always focused on me.

"I…um…" The bluntness of the kid was scary. "Who *are* you?"

"I am…" He pauses for a moment. "I am Nevian Cass."

I nod, swallowing hard. "What are you doing here, Nevian Cass?"

"I'm here to work for SCSS. Like you." His eyes finally left mine for a second to look at the door. "You don't have much time."

"What?"

Before he could answer, the door opened and Natalie stepped in, closing the door behind her.

Natalie frowns at me in disappointment. "Miles, did I not say, stay pu–"

"What is this?! Are you taking kids…and…and experimenting on them?!" I hissed, gesturing to the kids on the cots.

Natalie rubs her temples, "Miles, you need to leave before Kronos catches you."

I stuck my ground. "Natalie, what are you doing to these kids?!"

Natalie grabbed my arm, "Miles, you don't want to do this. These kids are going to be fine. They're new spies." She pulled me towards the door. "You have to leave. Now."

I glanced back at Nevian one more time before I walked out. I knew this wasn't the last time I'd be seeing him. Nevian locked eyes with me for a second and for a second, I thought I could hear his voice in the distance. Natalie shut the door behind her.

"Miles, what you did was extremely inappropriate. I told you to stay put but instead you did the opposite and wandered around - especially in a place like this!"

A place like this.

Child, be careful of SCSS.

You're not here because Kronos' wants to help you, but only to help himself.

"What do you mean 'a place like this'?"

Natalie looked unusually pale, and she caressed her temples as if she had a bad headache. "Miles, please just forget about this. You're not supposed to know about this."

"Well, I do, so might as well just tell me what's going on." I glanced over at my watch, seeing the countdown click to twenty minutes.

Natalie shook her head. "Drop this. Now, c'mon, get to your dorm. You failed your mission, you want to get another strike?"

I clenched my fists. "Fine." I walked over to the elevator and clicked the down button.

Natalie trailed after me, in silence. The door opened a second later and I hit floor four, the dorms.

She hit floor five for herself. A second later, she brought up a new subject. "Do you have anything you need to tell me?"

I froze. Did Natalie know I wasn't from his time period? How did she know? I really wanted to tell her. To tell her that Luke wasn't supposed to bring Aimee until months later, how the fifth floor wasn't supposed to be rearranged for another month, how I'm stuck in 2055, how nobody was coming to get me, how everything was moving…changing…how Nevian made my stomach do flips and turns, how Luca just disappeared…

I shook my head. "No. Nothing."

She nods. "Alright then. See you later." The door dings open and I linger a second then walk out.

Did I make the right decision?

The door seems to close in slow motion and soon Natalie is gone.

I sulked over to my dorm and opened the door. I looked up and froze when I saw him sitting on my bed.

☆ Introductions ☆

00:18:03

"Nevian?!" I stared at him in disbelief, how had he gotten here? And... so quickly?

"Hello, Miles. Nice to see you again." He looked up from the piece of paper he was studying.

"How did you get here?"

"Help from a friend, I suppose." He returns back to looking at the piece of paper. It had rows and rows of numbers.

"What friend?" I ask, utterly shocked.

"Oh, I'm sorry, I forgot to turn off the invisibility." A voice said, coming from behind me.

I jumped back, my hand going over to the taser on my belt.

In a flash, a tall guy maybe a few years older than me with blonde messy hair, hazel eye—

"Luca?" I mutter, shell-shocked.

Why was everybody surprising me today?

"Long time no see, huh?" He pats my back, laughing.

"How...?"

He laughs. "Long story. I heard you're in the wrong time period?"

Luca was still charming as ever. He was probably about twenty-two by now. His eyes were bright and curious and his smile lightened up the room, as cringey as it was to say.

"Miles being in this period is making the time periods mix up. The longer he is here, things start going wrong. At first it was small things - like the fifth floor being rearranged but next time it could be something bigger. That's why we need Miles out of this time period immediately." Nevian spoke up, looking up from his paper.

"What about...uh, if I stay here too long I'll die?"

Nevian nods. "I've weighed the instances of that happening. It's 50/50 as of now but of course it could change. Time is confusing." He looks back down.

I had so many questions like how Nevian knew so much about me and my situation and how Luca was back and how I had a fifty percent chance of dying. Still I held my questions in.

Luca chuckled. "Don't mind Nevian. I'm sure everything's going to be fine. We'll get you back to 2060 and hope everything reverses."

Ha. Hope? So whether I die or not it's all determined by how lucky I was? Bull.

Everyone was silent for a moment, lost in their own world. "So." I mumbled.

Nevian looked up. "What did Natalie say to you?"

I shrugged. "I wasn't supposed to be there or whatever." I looked back at my watch. 16 minutes remaining.

"When you were in the elevator."

I paused. How did he know? "She asked me if I wanted to say anything to her. I didn't say anything. Now can you stop...knowing everything?" It was creeping me out.

Nevian's eyes lingered me a second longer than normal before he looked away.

Luca rested a hand on my shoulder. "Want to know what happened after I left SCSS?"

I nod hesitantly.

Luca nodded and walked over to the couch. He patted the spot next to him. I sat. "The day I turned eighteen, Kronos' called me to his office. I hadn't expected any less. I knew what was happening. I'd be getting a check of money and a small ceremony, which I supposed he called 'graduation.' To the younger spies, it was a day to celebrate the spy who had completed their so-called 'spy training' and would be sent off to a higher, more skilled agency. But that wasn't the case at all and the older spies knew. They were next in line. After the 'graduation' the spy would have their memories erased and sent to anywhere in the world - even I don't know much about it but I know they experimented with people making it seem like that spy was with them their whole life. It's dirty. And evil." Luca paused, his face looking ghostly.

I swallowed hard, taking in everything Luca was saying.

"I don't know why, but Kronos called me into his office after the ceremony and I braced for my memory to be erased. But it never did. Instead, he gave me a check of 100,000, a boarding ticket across the world and an admission paper from one of the best schools in our time. He told me if I even breathed a word about SCSS to anybody...although he made it seem like it wasn't a threat, it very much was. And like that, I was shipped halfway across the world to go to college. I'm thankful, of course, because although SCSS made me street-smart, I was missing some of the book smart." He chuckled to himself.

He was right. Most spies at SCSS were street-smart, knowing what to do if anything happens in the world, fast reflexes, and persuading skills. And although all students had teachers that taught them math, science, English and the basics, it wasn't *enough*.

"Miles, the point is, Kronos lies. He doesn't want spies over eighteen because they're no longer children he could control. So he throws them back out on the streets. I knew you probably didn't understand before but I want you to understand now. You're not here because Kronos—"

"–Wants to help you but to help himself." I chuckled quietly. "Yeah, I remember that."

Luca smiled. "Yeah."

"But…if you went to college after SCSS how…how did you end up back here? In a time-zone you're not supposed to be in either?"

"See, this is what I haven't told you yet. While in college, I had extra time and I needed extra money. I don't know how they know me or how they know I worked at SCSS but an agency reached out to me. It's called Blake Rose Inc. They took me in as a new spy and they have so many gadgets including the invisibility cloak and a time belt."

"Wait, if you have a time belt, then we can just time travel back." I beamed, excitedly.

He shook his head, "it's not that simple. Each person has to have a time belt. Two people cannot go into the time chasm with one time belt. It will override and cause you to go somewhere in the void and it could be fatal."

"So, you're saying I'm never going to make it out of 2055?"

Luca sighed. "It's complicated but keep your head high. Just because something is complicated doesn't mean it's impossible. If things go really south, you'll use my time belt to get out of here by yourself."

"But what about you?"

He laughs. "Don't worry about me."

I frown. Luca was always like this. Putting people ahead of himself. Maybe that's what made him so likable.

Nevian got up from the bed and handed me the paper. I stared at it quizzically. "Those are the statistics of what could go wrong next."

I side-eyed him. Was this his way of showing off how smart he was? None of this made sense. Luca had a similar look on his face.

Nevian huffed a sigh. "It means the next situation that's moving up in the time-line is when Aimee malfunctions and the company shuts down for the day."

"But Aimee just came!" It was hard to wrap my head around everything that just happened.

Nevian had a small smirk on his face. "Isn't that what makes time so fascinating?

I exchanged a look with Luca, who looked more impressed than annoyed. "I don't know how Kronos did it, but it's amazing."

I looked at him curiously, "what do you mean?"

Luca looked over. "You didn't know?" He glanced over at Nevian and quietly said, "Nevian was experimented on with the factor of savant syndrome."

My eyebrows flew in surprise. "Savant syndrome? You mean that syndrome that makes you really smart? And…they experimented on him? A kid?"

Luca nodded. "It was a good discovery–"

"How are you going along with this?" I ask, in horror, "he's experimenting on poor innocent kids! How is that okay?"

Luca looked at me, with a kind of look I could distinguish. "Miles, I don't know if I've become desensitized or you really didn't know this…"

"Know what?" I demanded.

"Kronos experiments on everybody at SCSS. It's not just, oh, homeless kid on the road, let's bring him to SCSS! It's, homeless kid on the road, let's test him, and the strongest comes to SCSS."

"What do you mean the strongest?"

He sighs. "The one who is most mentally strong will proceed to live and work under Kronos. Those who are not so fortunate, don't make it…"

"Kronos kills people?!" I shriek.

Luca shushes me. "He doesn't keep mentally weak people. They're not beneficial…they're not *profitable*. This is business to him. Just keeping kids and providing them food, clothes, and a roof isn't exactly cheap. So he needs kids that are strong - not only physically but mentally as well - to do his work. I didn't think these experiments would get as big as this with savant syndrome. It's impressive if you think about it."

"So…I was experimented on? And you were too?"

He nods. "Just small things though. Although I'm not sure what kind of experiments he did, apparently we're extremely mentally smart."

"Is that why I can't remember a thing about my past?" Every time I tried to think of anything before the age five, I felt an excruciating pain in my head.

He nods. "I figured you'd know by now."

I shake my head. That makes a huge difference. Why every spy had photographic memory, why I couldn't think about my past, why Kronos never let us go to the seventh floor. The seventh floor was the lab.

I glanced over at Nevian. On the outside, he looked like a completely normal six or seven year old but on the inside, I could practically see the little wheels and rinds spinning in his brain.

Nevian stared blankly at me. "You're an interesting person. I can feel all your emotions." He reached up in the air, as if he was touching something. "Your emotions are powerful and I can feel them radiating in the air."

Luca nods. "Apparently, Nevian has another special ability. He can sense emotions like Kronos."

Huh. Well, I guess Nevian must be Kronos' favorite from the new spies.

Everyone was silent for a moment before Luca cleared his throat. "Well, I know you have a countdown so I suggest we get moving."

"Where are we going?"

"Up to the lab, of course. Kronos has more secrets to uncover." Luca smiled and tossed me a dark long cloak. "Put it on."

I obeyed and slipped the cloak on. "What does it do?"

Luca chuckled and even Nevian cracked a smile. "Look at your arm."

I looked down and…my arm was gone!

No, it wasn't gone. It was *invisible*. "Is this from your new agency?"

"Yeah. It wasn't too hard. All you need to do is manipulate the sun's rays and light around and instead direct to the cloak. It absorbs the light, taking away your shadow and figure. I'm sure Kronos has a prototype of that." Luca grabbed his own cloak and put it on. "C'mon, let's go."

"What about Nevian?" I ask.

Luca chuckles. "I'm not sure how he does it but I can guarantee he'll get there before us. Now just follow the slight air movements. That's me."

I nod, although he couldn't see me. I focused on the slight air movements that lead to the elevator and to the seventh floor.

The elevator stopped at the fifth floor. To my horror, Luke walked into the elevator and pressed the fourth floor.

I froze and I felt Luca press against me.

Even with the slight movement, I felt the air change.

Luke looked around in the elevator for a moment and it felt like he was staring right into my soul for a second before turning back to the elevator door.

The door ding opened and Luke slowly stepped out. He turned around to look back into the elevator, trying to see if anybody was there. Thankfully, he turned back around.

I blew out a breath I didn't realize I was holding. "That was close." I mumbled.

"Yeah...too close." Luca paused. "Who is he?"

"That's Luke...he joined SCSS not too long ago. Why?"

It felt like Luca shook his head. "Nothing. Doesn't he...doesn't he look like me?"

I paused. Luca and Luke. Blonde hair and although they had different color eyes you couldn't deny, the futures were similar.

But that wasn't possible, could it?

Luca was kind, smart and wise.

Luke didn't fill in any of the boxes.

I tried not to think about it as the elevator dinged open to the seventh floor and like said, Nevian was waiting for us.

Luca took off the cloak hood and I followed.

"Floating heads. Interesting." Nevian mused for a second before turning around and going back to the room I found him in.

Now that I could see clearly, there were about ten cots in the room. Each had a kid about Nevian's age that ranged between so many different races, colors, hair types, nationalities.

"Why are all these kids sleeping?" I ask Luca, looking up to see his face.

He had yet again an expressionless look on his face. "Hm? Sorry, I was just thinking about what happened earlier."

"What happened earlier?" Nevian blurted.

"He thinks one of the spies, Luke, is somehow related to him." I shrug. Although I doubted it, it was possible.

"Was Luke not the one who pushed you in the time chasm?" Nevian asked, studying my face again.

"Yeah." Clearly I still held a grudge against him and I definitely didn't want Luca to be around him. To twist his mind just like he does with everyone else.

Nevian nods. "It's possible." With that, he turns back around and looks at the rows of kids on the beds. "Each of them experimented with different things."

"Indeed. I knew someone was there."

We all spinned around to look at someone by the door. Luke.

☆ The Truth ☆

"What are you doing here, Luke?!" I ask, ridiculously.

"I should be asking you the same question." He noted, brushing off the dust of his suit.

I crossed my arms over my chest. "We have permission to be here. Unlike you."

"Hey, hey, why so much negative energy?" Luke chuckles.

I looked away. I needed to remember this was not the Luke who got me in this mess. This was past Luke. Then why did he look so smug?

Luke quietly examined the room, then looked over at Nevian who stared back, and finally his eyes landed on Luca. His eyes slightly widened.

I stepped in front of Luca, a feeling of jealousy washing over me. Luke stepped back.

Luca quietly ran his eyes over Luke. It was undeniable. The similarities were there.

But so were the differences.

Luca was tall, with long built arms and long legs. Luca had hazel eyes while Luke had blue.

"What's your last name?" Luca asked, suddenly.

"Vladamiser." Luke fumbled out.

"That's my last name too."

Everybody paused for a second before Nevian started rambling about how it's definitely possible.

So. I guess they really are brothers.

There was still a slight chance that they weren't but that chance is thinner than a strand of hair.

Luca looked over at my face and set a hand on my shoulder. It was supposed to be reassuring but it felt more like he was pitying me.

I shrugged off his hand gently and turned back to Nevian. "Do any of your statistics tell me when Luke *leaves*?"

Nevian shakes his head and glances over at Luca and Luke, talking quietly. "C'mon, let's take a walk."

I roll my eyes but Nevian grabs my hand and leads me out the door. I grab the cloak on the way out.

I probably needed that walk because to tell the truth I was angry. I was angry at the fact that Luke could get whatever he wants. And not just items or day-offs. He could get people on his side. He gaslights. He manipulates. He guilt-trips. He's evil.

And even after all that, everybody likes him. Except me. But it was pretty mutual.

Nevian still tightly holds my hand as we explore the seventh floor. His tight hold was somehow comforting and it made me a little less angry.

As we looked around, the rest of the rooms were locked and lined with a silver lining that probably was electric. What *was* in those rooms?

Nevian had a similar expression on his face. Each door we passed was the same. Locked and barbed. Until we got to the last door in the hallway.

I picked up Nevian and hid him under my cloak and we quietly scattered inside the room.

Completely different from the other room we were in, it was dark and quiet with no windows.

I felt around the wall for a light-switch. I quickly flipped it on when I found it. It was still dim but we could see. There were tables with at least five computers on-top. Nevian quickly ran over and started them up.

Immediately they flashed to hundreds of recordings. It was a monitor. Nevian clicked some keys and soon, we were seeing camera footage from a few minutes ago. It was Kronos' office.

Him, Natalie and Luke were circled around his desk and there sat a USB that was probably Aimee.

Luke had a smug look on his face. "Kronos, Natalie, may I present you, AI899, who we call AIMEE."

Kronos seemed impressed. "Thank you, Mr. Vladmiser. We'll set her up all around SCSS."

A dumb part of me thought *even the bathrooms?*

I quickly shooed the thought away. Aimee wasn't in the bathrooms. Was she?

"Luke, we appreciate your discovery and your accomplishment will not go unseen. You're free of any missions for a bit and remember, if you need anything, ask Natalie. Enjoy yourself."

Luke had the smuggest smile I'd ever seen in my life and he stared over at the camera direction as if he knew I was watching. His smile probably said; *ha! I'm better than you! Look how hopeless and pathetic you look.* Or something similar to that.

Nevian moved away from the screen and looked around. There was not much to see.

I went back to the footage from yesterday and I saw Tala, Mae and Taj in Kronos' office.

They were talking rather quietly and I had to put the sound to the max.

"--I need you three to keep your distance away from Miles."

My eyebrows raised. Why would Kronos say that?"

They nodded in unison and quickly added, "yes, sir."

"Nevian." I mumble.

Nevian appeared by my side, glancing at my face then back at the screen. His small hand slipped in mine.

"Sir, if I may–" Mae tried to add but Tala stopped her.

Kronos nods, letting Mae continue.

"Sir, I would just like to know why…I mean, we're all roommates."

Kronos nods, his eyes slightly dancing with amusement once more. "That's for me to know and you to find out, Miss Mae." Then he nodded towards the door.

Mae nodded and everybody left the room. Then the camera cut.

Nevian squeezed my hand reassuringly. "Would you like to go back?"

I turn off the computer. "Could we go to Kronos' office?"

"Why?"

I shrug. I needed to confront him about all the secrets he was keeping. Why he was experimenting on children. Everything. "I just wanna ask him a few questions."

"What about Luca and Luke?"

"They'll be fine. You wanna come?"

Nevian nods.

I hid Nevian under my cloak and quickly left the room, leaving it like we found it.

We slipped into the elevator and pressed floor five, hoping nobody comes in.

Thankfully, nobody came in and I quickly gave Nevian the cloak. "Wait by the door for me."

He nods.

I step out of the elevator. Natalie's by her desk again. She gives me a pointed look.

"Can I go in?"

She nods.

I give her a half-hearted smile before knocking on Kronos' door. A 'come in' came from him and I walked in.

Kronos looks up from his computer, his eyebrows raising slightly. "Hello, Miles."

"Hi, sir."

He analyzes me quickly. "Is there anything you need, Mr. Miles, showing up unannounced?"

"Ah, yes, sir. I have some questions, if I may."

He nods.

"If there's face recognition on the portal, how did I get in?"

He sighs. "It was working, just not particularly well, I suppose." He looks over, "do you think there's a deeper explanation?"

"There's always a deeper explanation. Just like SCSS."

Kronos narrows his eyes slightly. "What do you mean by that?"

"The deer's in the park warned me about you. And SCSS."

"The deer's don't know what they're talking about. They're deer's for god's sake." Kronos spat.

I shrugged. "They seem to know what they're talking about."

Kronos looked up and his eyes met mine and a chill went down my spine. "SCSS holds many secrets but it being a bad organization isn't one of them. Must I remind you where you were before I–"

Ha. He was gaslighting. "I appreciate the act of kindness you did for me, but I don't believe you did it for me but for your own benefit."

"Miles, I don't know who's feeding you this information, but I trusted you were not idiotic enough to believe it."

I clenched my fists. I didn't say anything, not wanting to make him angrier.

"Is this what you wanted to ask me?" He asks, regaining his composure.

I swallowed hard. "No, sir. I have a few more."

Every part of me wanted to turn around and go back to my dorm but my heart told me I had to. I had to find out what made SCSS so chilling. "Why do you experiment on us? On young kids? Are we just toys for you?"

Kronos chuckled a chuckle that had no humor in it. Instead, it made my skin crawl. "I see you've been exploring places you shouldn't be in."

I didn't agree nor deny.

He nods. "Miles, let me tell you something. Secrets in SCSS are there for reasons. Like cameras and security. Not everything can be open and free. Or else chaos would wreak havoc."

"Why not be honest with your spies so you feel at least morally gray?" I blurted.

Kronos said nothing but I could tell the comment stuck to him.

I had more questions, but I could tell he wasn't going to give any answers. "Well. I'll be heading out then."

I reached for the doorknob.

"Wait."

I turned around.

"Miles, I'd like to tell you something." He began after a long pause.

I waited for him to go on, my heart skipping a beat when I saw there was one minute left on my clock.

"I'm your father."

www.ingramcontent.com/pod-product-compliance
Lightning Source LLC
Chambersburg PA
CBHW050834180626
46814CB00004B/1620